A roug...

Puddles rode so s... ..., I felt like I was floating. I watched the trees and the fence posts spin by as we rode around and around. Before I knew it, I was day-dreaming.

I was still daydreaming when I heard the buzzing sound again. I looked down and saw the bee. This time it was on Puddles's neck. I reached out my hand to brush it away. . . .

The next thing I knew, Puddles let out a high-pitched whinny and reared backward. I felt myself flying into the air. For a moment all I could see was the sky, and then I hit the ground.

Bantam Books in the SWEET VALLEY KIDS series

SWEET VALLEY KIDS

ELIZABETH'S HORSEBACK ADVENTURE

Written by
Molly Mia Stewart

Created by
FRANCINE PASCAL

Illustrated by
Ying-Hwa Hu

BANTAM BOOKS
NEW YORK · TORONTO · LONDON · SYDNEY · AUCKLAND

RL 2, 005-008

ELIZABETH'S HORSEBACK ADVENTURE
A Bantam Book / January 1996

Sweet Valley High® and Sweet Valley Kids® are
registered trademarks of Francine Pascal

Conceived by Francine Pascal

Produced by Daniel Weiss Associates, Inc.
33 West 17th Street
New York, NY 10011

Cover art by Susan Tang

ISBN: 0-553-48217-3

Published simultaneously in the United States and Canada

Bantam Books are published by Bantam Books, a division of Bantam
Doubleday Dell Publishing Group, Inc. Its trademark, consisting of the
words "Bantam Books" and the portrayal of a rooster, is Registered in the
U.S. Patent and Trademark Office and in other countries. Marca
Registrada. Bantam Books, 1540 Broadway, New York, New York 10036.

PRINTED IN THE UNITED STATES OF AMERICA

OPM   0 9 8 7 6 5 4 3 2 1

To Brandon Benjiman Allen

CHAPTER 1
The Horse Show

Hi! My name is Elizabeth Wakefield. I'm seven years old and so is my sister, Jessica. People confuse me with her all the time. I can't really blame them, since Jessica and I are identical twins. We both have blond hair with bangs, and blue-green eyes. Sometimes even our mom and dad have a hard time telling us apart!

But usually it's not so hard, because Jessica is really different from me. She likes to play dress-up and hates to get even the tiniest bit of dirt on her clothes. I'd rather go horseback riding or play soccer on the Sweet Valley Elementary team, and I don't mind getting my clothes muddy.

Jessica hates school. The only things she likes about it are recess and talking with her friends. I love to read, and I think it's fun to learn new things. We're so different, I bet if we didn't look the same, nobody would guess we're related.

Even though we don't agree all the time, we agree on the important things, like which kind of ice cream we like in our sundaes. We fight sometimes, but we always make up. I feel very lucky to have a twin sister, and Jessica does, too.

One afternoon at recess, my friend Amy Sutton and I were standing by the swings, talking about our horseback-riding lessons. Ever since we'd heard about the big horse show coming up, we hardly talked about anything else.

"I can't believe we only have two weeks to get ready for the show!" Amy Sutton said. She sat on a swing and pushed off as hard as she could.

"Me, neither!" I said.

"What show?" Lila Fowler asked as she and Jessica walked toward us. Lila was scowling. She hates being left out of anything.

"The Happy Hoofs Horse Show!" Amy said. "Elizabeth and I are both going to be in it!"

"Horses," Lila said. "That's all you two ever talk about."

"I think horses are cool!" Jessica said. "Remember when I rode a horse in the circus?"

"Uh-huh," Lila said with a yawn. "You talked about it for three weeks straight."

I got on the swing next to Amy and tried to go as high as she was going. "We get to put on our best riding clothes and parade in front of everyone," I said. "Mom and Dad will be there, and my grandparents, and even Great-aunt Helen. She's the one who got me the riding lessons as a present."

"My aunt got me sneakers as a present, but you don't hear me talking about it," Lila said. "Anyway, horses are big and smelly."

"Who's big and smelly? Besides you?" said a voice behind us. We turned around and saw Jerry McAllister, the class bully, leaning against the swings and smirking at us.

"Very funny," Amy said. "Actually, we were talking about horses."

"Horses? Yeeha!" Jerry bent over and pretended to be a cowboy riding the range. "Giddyap! Hi-ho, Silver!"

"Jerry, you're such a pain," Jessica said. "I bet you can't even ride."

"Sure I can," Jerry said. "It's easy."

"Have you ever done it before?" Lila asked.

"Naw." Jerry snorted. "Why bother? It must be easy, if girls can do it."

"You're just a chicken," Jessica said.

"I am not!" Jerry yelled.

Amy laughed. "I bet the horse would throw you, just to get you off his back."

Jerry's face turned red. "Why am I wasting my time with you wimpy girls anyway?" he said, and walked away.

Amy and I rolled our eyes at each other. "Who cares what Jerry thinks?" I said. "Just wait till the horse show. We'll show him who's wimpy."

CHAPTER 2

Hello, Puddles

Mrs. Sutton gave Amy and me a ride to the stables after school that day for our riding lessons.

"You girls have a good time, now," Mrs. Sutton said. "And be careful, Amy."

Amy made a face. Mrs. Sutton always tells her to be careful. "I will, Mom. Don't worry."

"Thanks for the ride, Mrs. Sutton," I said.

"You're welcome," she said.

Amy and I ran toward the barn. I could smell the horses already. I was getting excited, like I always do when we're about to ride.

"Hi, Amy! Hi, Elizabeth!" Becky, our riding instructor, called as she came out of the stables. Becky is seventeen and has long, straight dark hair. She always wears a bandanna tied around her neck. I like her a lot.

"Are you ready to ride?" Becky asked.

"I can't wait!" Amy said. "The show's only two weeks away. I need to practice!"

"Me, too!" I said.

"OK, then, let's go!" Becky said. "Amy, I'll help you tack up Juniper. Elizabeth, Puddles is all saddled and ready to go. Why don't you put on your riding hat, then take him out back and warm him up?"

"Sure!" I said. I like tacking up—putting on the saddle and reins and stuff—but it's even more fun to start riding right away. I felt especially excited that Becky was letting me take Puddles out all by myself. *I'm getting to be a good rider,* I thought proudly.

I took my riding hat from its hook and fastened it securely to my head. Then I went to check on Puddles. His stall was the last one in the barn. "Hello, boy," I said. I patted his nose.

Puddles is just about the most beautiful horse in the world. He's a pretty pale gray horse with snowy white hoofs. When I came near him, I could see his eyes light right up. He likes me a lot.

Suddenly I heard a buzzing noise in my ears. It was a bee flying around my head. I swatted it away. "Don't let that bee bother you, Puddles. Let's go stretch your legs."

I took hold of Puddles's reins and unlatched the gate to his stall. We walked out into the fenced-in riding ring behind the barn. Beyond the fence was a big grassy field. Part of it was wide-open, and part of it had fences for the advanced riding students to jump over. Way off in the distance I could see hills all the way to the horizon.

"Whoa, boy," I told Puddles. "Hold still while I climb on."

Puddles stopped. He's a good horse, and he always does what I ask him to do. I stood on his left side and put my left foot in the stirrup. Then I jumped up and swung my right leg over his back so that I was perched in the saddle. "Good boy, Puddles," I said, patting his neck.

I love being on Puddles's back, way up high in the air. It makes me feel like I'm on top of the world and nothing can hurt me. "OK, Puddles," I said. "Let's trot."

I nudged him in the side a little with the heels of my boots and flicked the reins. Puddles started trotting in a slow circle around the ring.

I heard the buzzing sound again. The bee had followed us right out of the barn. "Can't you take a hint?" I said to the bee, shooing it away again.

Puddles rode so smoothly, I felt like I was floating. I watched the trees and the fence posts spin by as we rode around and around. Before I knew it, I was daydreaming. I pictured myself standing on a winner's podium in my best riding uniform as a judge handed me a shiny blue ribbon. "First place!" he said in a booming voice. Then he took a big wreath of roses and put it around Puddles's neck. Puddles looked as proud as I did.

I was still daydreaming when I heard

the buzzing sound again. I looked down and saw the bee. This time it was on Puddles's neck. I reached out my hand to brush it away. . . .

The next thing I knew, Puddles let out a high-pitched whinny and reared backward. I felt myself flying into the air. For a moment all I could see was the sky, and then I hit the ground.

CHAPTER 3

Just a Little Accident

The wind was knocked out of me at once. I lay gasping on the ground. Puddles reared back on his hind legs and neighed. From the ground he looked enormous to me, like a big-toothed monster.

I tried to move, but I couldn't. I was terrified. Puddles just kept kicking the air and whinnying. *He's going to trample me!* I thought miserably.

I squeezed my eyes shut and shivered. I didn't want to see what was going to happen next.

"Puddles! Stop it!" It was Becky's

voice. "Whoa, Puddles, down! *Down!*"

When I opened my eyes, Becky had got ahold of Puddles's reins. He was back on all fours, pacing. He almost looked normal again.

"Elizabeth!" Becky cried. She leaned down beside me. "Are you all right?"

I was having trouble breathing. I tried to talk, but no words came out, so I just nodded.

"Thank goodness. Just lie still," she told me. "You'll get your breath back in a minute."

She was right. The more I calmed down, the easier it was to breathe. Then I glanced up at Puddles. He looked bigger than I remembered. Had I actually ridden something so high up?

Amy ran up leading Juniper behind her. She had a worried look on her face. "Liz! Are you all right?"

"I-I think so," I said.

"That was a bad fall," Becky said to me. "Does anything feel broken?"

I shook my head. "I think I'm OK. Can you help me up?"

Amy and Becky each grabbed one arm and lifted me up. "See?" I said. "No problem."

Becky still looked worried. "But you're shaking," she said.

"What?"

"Look at your hands." She pointed.

I looked. My hands *were* shaking.

"You don't *look* hurt," Becky said, "but just to be safe, we'll call off your lesson for today. I want you to get a drink of water and sit down awhile, OK?"

"OK," I said.

"Good," Becky said. "I'll take Puddles to his stall. Then I'll call your mom and tell her what happened."

Becky took Puddles by the reins and

16

walked him back inside. I made sure I kept my distance from him.

Amy grabbed my hand. "I was so scared," she said. "But you were really brave! You could have been killed!"

I bit my lip. "It's no big deal," I said. But I knew it was.

For the rest of the lesson I watched Amy ride Juniper. I felt a little sore, but I wasn't really hurt. Mostly just shaken up.

I was sitting on the fence when I saw Mom's car pull up. She jumped out and ran over to me. She gave me a big hug.

"Elizabeth! Are you all right?" she asked.

"I'm fine, Mom," I said. "Except you're kinda crushing me."

"Sorry, honey," Mom said. "But I was so worried. Becky said you'd been thrown by a horse!"

"It was just a little accident," I explained. I didn't want Mom to worry. "I'm not even hurt. See?"

She squeezed me again. "As long as you're in one piece," she said. "Come on, let's go home."

I called to Amy, and the three of us walked to the car. All the way home I tried to relax, but I couldn't stop thinking of something Amy had said: *You could have been killed.*

CHAPTER 4
A Nightmare Horse

That night at the dinner table, Mom told the rest of the family about my accident. They looked really surprised.

"Are you sure you're all right, Elizabeth?" Dad asked. "You must have been frightened."

"I'm fine," I said. "It wasn't a big deal or anything."

Even my older brother, Steven, who usually likes to make fun of me and Jessica, looked a little worried about me. "Your horse must have been really mad at you," he said. "What did you do to it?"

"Nothing! Puddles didn't throw me on purpose," I said. "He likes me. He'd never do anything to hurt me." At least, I didn't *think* he would.

"Yeah, be quiet," Jessica said. "You don't know *anything* about horses."

"Like you do," Steven muttered. He turned back to me. "Are you gonna quit your lessons?" he asked.

I thought about that for a few seconds. "No," I said. "Not with the horse show coming up and everything. I don't want to disappoint Great-aunt Helen."

Dad smiled. "I don't think you could *ever* disappoint Great-aunt Helen," he said. "But I'm sure she'll be very proud to see you ride."

"I'd quit if I were you," Steven said. "Maybe next time that horse will trample you."

I tried to ignore him, but I couldn't stop the shiver creeping up my spine.

*　　　*　　　*

"Were you really scared?" Jessica whispered to me later that night. It was almost time to go to sleep. We were sitting on our twin beds in our favorite teddy-bear pajamas.

"Maybe a little," I said. I bit my fingernail. "Well, more than a little."

"I fell off my bed once," Jessica said.

"It's not really the same thing," I said. "A horse is much higher up, and it was moving."

"Sounds awful," Jessica said.

"It was," I said.

"Hey, cowgirls," Dad said, coming into the room with Mom. "Time for bed."

They tucked us in and kissed us good night. Dad turned off the light and closed the bedroom door behind him.

"Puddles wouldn't hurt you, right?" Jessica whispered in the darkness. "You said so yourself."

"Right," I finally said. "There's nothing to worry about."

"I'm glad," Jessica said. "Night."

"Night."

It took me a while to fall asleep. Some of the muscles in my back were still sore from the fall. Finally I dozed off. . . .

Suddenly I was back in the ring at the stables. It was late at night, and I couldn't see a thing, not even my own feet. As I walked, my boots thumped loudly on the ground. I was trying to open the gate to get out of the ring, but it wouldn't budge.

Then I heard something. It was a buzzing noise, like a bee, but a lot louder. It sounded like a chain saw, and it was coming closer and closer.

That's when I saw two points of light in the distance. They were red, like hot iron. I heard the sound of clattering hooves, even louder than the buzzing noise. The red lights raced toward me. I realized they were eyes—the eyes of a horse.

Then all at once I could see him: It was Puddles, and he was charging toward me. His coat was black as night, and he breathed fire. He looked like he wanted to kill me!

I turned and ran as fast as I could. I kept looking over my shoulder and saw that Puddles was catching up with me. Sparks flew from his hooves every time they struck the ground. He was a monster horse!

It was no use, I couldn't outrun him. One last time I turned to look. Puddles was practically right on top of me. I screamed as loud as I could. . . .

Then I woke up.

The blankets were all twisted around my body, and I could feel the sweat trickling down my back. Jessica was still fast asleep. I was glad. I didn't want anyone to know about my nightmare.

But I made a decision right then and there. I was never going to ride a horse again.

CHAPTER 5

Harder Than It Looks

I couldn't fall back to sleep that night. So I got up early, before Steven and Jessica even opened their eyes. When I came into the kitchen, Mom and Dad were drinking coffee and talking.

"Elizabeth," Mom said. "What are you doing up so early?"

"I had a nightmare," I told her, twisting the hem of my pajama top around my fingers. "It was awful." I paused, trying to think of the best way to say what I had to say. "W-would you be disappointed in me if I gave up riding lessons?"

Mom and Dad looked at each other for a moment. "I guess you had a bigger scare than you thought, huh?" Dad asked.

I shrugged. "Guess so," I said, looking down.

Mom came over and put her arm around me. "Are you sure you want to stop?" she asked. "I thought you loved to ride."

I stared at the floor tiles, feeling ashamed. "I *do* love to ride," I said. "But I'm scared of getting hurt."

Mom gave me a kiss on the cheek. "I'll tell you what," she said. "Why don't you keep going for your lessons and try to get back on the horse? After a few times, if you still want to give it up, you can. OK?"

I winced. "I don't know. . . ."

"The only way to get over being scared," Dad said, "is to face up to what you're afraid of."

27

"I'm sure you can do it," Mom added.

I wasn't so sure, but it seemed like a fair deal. So I said OK.

"Good!" Mom said. She gave me a big hug. "Now, how about your favorite breakfast—blueberry pancakes?"

"Great!" I said. Suddenly I felt so happy, I forgot all about horses.

Later that morning, I was sitting in my second-grade classroom waiting for Mrs. Otis to come in and take attendance, when I heard Amy's voice behind me.

"Elizabeth had a terrible fall yesterday!"

"Off a horse?" Lila asked, looking right at me.

"Uh-huh," I mumbled. This was the last thing I felt like talking about, but Amy kept going.

"A bee stung her horse, and he threw

her to the ground! She could have been killed!" Amy practically shouted.

"I wish you'd stop saying that," I said. It was really making me jittery.

Before Amy could say anything else, Jessica jumped in and interrupted her.

"It's true, she *could* have been killed!" Jessica said. "Her horse threw her almost twenty feet! Then he almost trampled her!"

"That's not true!" I said. "You weren't even there!"

But Jessica wasn't listening. A few of the other kids had heard what she'd said. They were starting to gather around, and Jessica was enjoying the attention.

"But my sister wasn't scared!" Jessica said. "She's tough—like me!"

I elbowed my sister. "Jess, keep it down!" I whispered. "I don't want everybody to—"

Just then, Caroline Pearce stepped right between our desks. She's a snoop and a tattletale. She's *always* putting her nose where it doesn't belong.

"You don't want everybody to what?" she asked.

"Elizabeth got thrown by a horse yesterday," Jessica said before I could stop her.

"Cool!" Caroline said. Then she skipped away with a smug grin on her face.

"Great!" I said. "Now she'll tell everyone! In about ten minutes the whole *school* will know!"

"So what?" Jessica said.

"Forget it," I muttered.

"If I were you, I'd give up those riding lessons," Lila said. "I mean, it's not worth getting killed just to ride some smelly horse around a ring."

"No way!" Amy said. Her eyes

opened wide. "Elizabeth would *never* give up riding. Any real cowgirl knows how to take a fall."

"And especially not with Grandma and Grandpa and Great-aunt Helen coming to watch her in the show," Jessica said.

I swallowed hard. I didn't know what to say.

Luckily, at that moment, Mrs. Otis came into the room carrying her briefcase. "Good morning, class!" she said.

"Good morning, Mrs. Otis!" we all said.

Just as I was pulling my pencils and notebook out of my backpack, I heard someone say "Psst!" I turned and saw Jerry McAllister sneering at me.

"Be careful you don't fall out of your chair, wimp," he said. "I hear sitting down is a *lot* harder than it looks."

A couple of boys heard what he said. They laughed.

I felt my heart sink. Maybe I really was a wimp.

CHAPTER 6
Still Spooked

On Saturday it was time for my next riding lesson. I'd been dreading it for days. My stomach was doing cartwheels as Mom drove Amy and me to the stables.

"Have fun, girls," she said when she dropped us off. "Sweetheart, I'm very proud of you," she said to me after Amy had jumped out of the car. "You're very brave."

I swallowed hard and tried to smile. "Thanks, Mom," I said.

For the first time since I'd started taking lessons, I felt more nervous than excited as I walked toward the barn. The smell of the horses made my stomach bunch up in knots. But I'd promised Mom I'd try to ride, and I wanted to keep my promise.

Becky met us in front of the barn. "Hi, girls," she said. "How are both my blue-ribbon winners today?"

I blinked. "But we haven't won any blue ribbons," I said.

"Just a matter of time," Becky said. "But we only have a few more lessons left till the show. Come on, let's bring our horses around to the front."

Amy ran right to her horse and started getting him ready. Just a few days before, I would have done the same thing. But now I dragged my feet as slowly as possible.

Puddles was in his stall. He looked the same as ever—not at all like a nightmare horse. Still, I didn't want to get too close to him.

Puddles looked so big to me now. I barely came up to his chest! Why do horses do what people want them to do, when they are so much stronger than people? I couldn't believe I'd ever ridden Puddles. How could I have controlled an animal so huge?

When Puddles saw me, his big eyes seemed to fill with guilt. I could see he felt sorry for throwing me.

"That's OK, Puddles," I said. "I know you didn't do it on purpose."

But how could I know that? After all, Puddles was a *horse*. It wasn't like I could know for sure. He certainly couldn't tell me.

This is silly, I told myself. *Don't be such a chicken. You know how to ride a horse. You've done it tons of times. So what are you afraid of?*

I had almost convinced myself I was ready to ride again, when Puddles moved his head and tried to nudge me

with his nose. It startled me and I jumped back. My pulse was pounding. Then I realized Puddles was just trying to be affectionate. I really was a chicken.

"Elizabeth? Are you coming?"

It was Becky calling from outside. She and Amy were all saddled up and ready to ride. I walked over to Becky's horse. I felt ashamed of myself, but I knew what I was going to say.

"Uh . . . I don't feel very good today, Becky," I said. "I think I'd better sit out until I feel better."

Becky looked down at me. I think she could see how spooked I was. She smiled in a sad but understanding way.

"OK," she said. "We don't want our star rider feeling sick. You can ride whenever you feel ready. OK?"

"Thanks, Becky," I said.

Amy was staring down at me from her horse. She had a puzzled look on her face. It made me uncomfortable.

"OK, Amy, let's ride," Becky said. She snapped her reins, and they both rode off.

I wandered around the stables. Out in the ring behind the barn, I saw another girl getting a riding lesson. She was a year or two younger than I was and had black hair pulled back with a bright yellow scrunchy. She was sitting on a huge black Thoroughbred, which her instructor led around the ring. The girl was jumping up and down in the saddle, looking very excited. "When can we start jumping the fences?" she asked. Her instructor just smiled.

The girl looked so tiny on that Thoroughbred's back. I wondered if she'd ever get hurt by *her* horse. I turned away.

Just before I left, I looked inside the stable to see how Puddles was doing. His head was bowed, and he looked sad.

CHAPTER 7

Elizabeth the Chicken

In the car on the way home, I didn't tell Mom that I hadn't done any riding. When she asked me how the lesson went, I just told her it went fine.

"That's great!" she said. She squeezed my arm. "I knew you could do it."

Amy gave me another strange look, but she didn't say anything. I was relieved.

Maybe next time I'll have the nerve to tell Mom, I thought. *Or maybe I'll even feel like riding again. Who knows?*

*   *   *

On Monday morning, Jessica and I were sharing a seat on the school bus. Amy was talking with Caroline Pearce a few rows ahead of us. I saw Amy whisper something in Caroline's ear. Then Caroline's mouth dropped wide-open.

"Wonder what that blabbermouth Caroline is up to now," Jessica murmured.

"I don't know," I said. "And I don't want to know."

Amy wouldn't tell Caroline about Saturday, I thought. *Would she?*

Caroline turned in her seat to look back at me. She smirked. Then she turned away.

Mrs. Otis taught us about fractions that morning. I had a good time. But when recess came, the fun was over.

I was swinging with Amy, Jessica,

and Lila. Suddenly I heard a buzzing sound. I looked down and saw a yellow-and-black insect crawling up my shirt.

"A bee!" I shrieked.

"That's not a bee," Amy said calmly. "It's a wasp. I think there's a nest nearby."

"It's going to sting me!" I yelled.

"Hold still," Amy said.

Amy reached out and brushed the wasp off my clothes. It buzzed up and out of sight. I calmed down.

"It was probably more afraid of you than you were of it," Amy told me. "After all, you're a lot bigger than a wasp."

"Yeah, but people don't go around stinging wasps," Jessica said. "Are you OK, Elizabeth?"

I noticed that my jaw was trembling. I bit down on my cheek to stop it. "Yeah," I said.

"Whatsamatter, fraidy-cat?"

I turned and saw the last person I wanted to see: Jerry McAllister. He looked even more pleased with himself than usual. "Are you scared of *all* animals now?"

"Wh-what do you mean by that?" I asked.

"Oh, nothing," he said. "You know, I can *almost* understand a girl being afraid of a big bad horse. But a teensy-weensy bee? Come *on*."

"What are you talking about?" Jessica said. "Liz isn't afraid of horses. She rides every week!"

"Not anymore," Jerry said. "I hear that ever since her fall, she's too scared to even get in the saddle."

I gave Amy an angry look. Amy looked over at Caroline. Caroline shrugged and ran off to play on the swings.

"Amy, why did you tell her?" I asked.

Amy looked very guilty. "You didn't tell me not to!" she said. "Besides, Caroline promised she wouldn't tell anybody!"

I felt awful. So awful, I felt like I had to lie—again.

"It's not true!" I yelled at Jerry. "I just felt sick on Saturday! I'm not afraid of horses!"

"Sure, whatever you say," Jerry said. "Chicken."

I thought I might burst into tears right there. But then Jessica came to my rescue. She grabbed Jerry by the arm.

"Hey!" she said. "*Nobody* calls my sister a chicken! Wait till *you* get thrown by a horse! Then we'll see how much *you* feel like riding!"

"Let go of me!" Jerry said.

"You apologize to my sister!" Jessica insisted.

The recess bell rang. Jerry yanked

45

his arm out of Jessica's grip. Then he cracked his knuckles.

"It's a good thing for you I don't have time to pound you," he said before he walked away.

Jessica made two fists and shook them at Jerry's back. "*Now* who's a chicken?" she cried.

Everyone was heading back inside for class. Even though my secret was out, I didn't feel completely awful. After all, at least Jessica had stood up for me.

"Forget him, Jess. Let's go in," I said.

Jessica lowered her fists. "OK," she said, but she wasn't smiling. The second bell rang before I could ask her what was wrong.

CHAPTER 8

The Girl in the Mirror

For the rest of the school day, I wondered what was bothering Jessica. She looked so worried. She didn't even talk and pass notes during class, like she usually does.

Jessica was still staring off into space when we got off the school bus that afternoon. I wanted to thank her for standing up for me, so I opened my mouth to say something—but Jessica beat me to it.

"Why didn't you *say* you were afraid of horses?" she said. It was almost like she was angry at me.

I was so surprised, at first I couldn't think of a thing to say. "I—I don't know," I stammered.

"How come you told Amy, but you didn't tell me?" Jessica sounded hurt.

"I didn't tell her!" I said. "I didn't tell anybody. Amy was at my lesson with me. She figured it out for herself!"

"Oh," Jessica said. "Well, next time you have a secret, just remember to tell me first. After all, I am your twin sister."

"OK," I said, smiling at her.

We walked together in silence toward our house. Jessica still seemed to be distracted.

"What are you thinking about?" I finally asked her.

Jessica stopped. She whirled around to face me. "You're not going to give up riding, are you?" she asked.

I nibbled my lower lip. "I don't

know," I said. "Do you think I should?"

"No, I don't," Jessica said firmly. "You're not a chicken! Besides, what about Great-aunt Helen coming to see you in the show?"

"I know," I said worriedly. "But after I fell off Puddles, I had this awful nightmare. Ever since then I've been terrified of my own horse."

Jessica looked at me strangely. "You're having *nightmares*?"

Now I was getting angry. Jessica was making me feel like a scared little baby! "I can't help it," I said. "I don't want to get thrown again."

Jessica shook her head. "You *have* to get back in the saddle, Liz. You can't let some dumb bad dream make you stop."

I felt my face get hot. "You think I'm a coward, too, don't you? Just like Jerry!"

"I didn't say that," Jessica said. "I just—"

I thought I was going to cry. I covered my face with my hands and ran toward the house. Now even my own sister thought I was chicken! And I thought she was on *my* side!

When I got inside the house, I ran right up to our bedroom and closed the door. I sat on the bed and cried. *Maybe Jess is right,* I thought. *Maybe I am just a big baby.*

I heard Mom knocking on the door. "Elizabeth?" she said.

I tried to calm down. I kept my voice really steady.

"Yes, Mom?"

"Are you all right, honey?" Mom asked. "May I come in?"

I felt awful, lying to Mom again. But I knew if I didn't, I'd have to tell her everything.

"I'm fine," I said. "I'll come

downstairs in a little while, OK?"

I didn't hear anything for a second. Then Mom said, "All right, Elizabeth," and I heard her walk away.

I went into the bathroom and washed my face with cold water. When I looked in the mirror, I didn't like the girl I saw. Not only was she a coward, but she lied, too. To her own mother.

"I've got to do something," I said. But I didn't know what.

CHAPTER 9
Jake

On Wednesday, Mom dropped Amy and me off at the stables. Amy was kind of quiet.

"I'm sorry I told Caroline," she said in a soft voice.

I shrugged. "It's OK. No big deal."

"It's going to be lonesome riding in the show without you," she said.

"What do you mean? I am going to ride in the show," I said. But I didn't sound too convincing.

Becky came out and said hello to us. "Do you feel like riding today, Elizabeth?" she asked.

"Um, not yet," I said. "I think I'll watch for a while."

Becky sighed. "All right. Puddles would probably like to see you. He's all tacked up and ready to go, in case you change your mind. Amy, let's go get ready for the show."

I went into the stable to say hi to Puddles. He still looked gigantic to me, but at least he didn't look like a monster. He seemed a little sad with his saddle on, stuck in the stall with nowhere to go.

"Hi, big boy," I said. "Sorry I'm such a wimp."

Puddles didn't seem to mind. He nudged me hello with his nose. I started to feel like I might be able to trust him again. I'd brought an apple with me. I took it out of my pocket and fed it to him. He ate it up in two bites.

Outside, I heard some shouting. I went out to see what was happening.

Out on the jump course, a teenage boy with short brown hair was riding a white Thoroughbred. A bunch of riders his age were standing by the barn, cheering him on.

"Come on, Jake!" they called. "Show us how it's done!"

Jake waved to them and smiled. Then he nudged his horse, and it took off like a shot. Jake and his horse went over six high fences like it was the easiest thing in the world. The boy and his horse looked like they were flying.

"All right!" his friends cheered. "Way to go!"

I cheered right along with them. Jake was about the best rider I'd ever seen.

A little while later, I decided to brush Puddles's coat. I got inside the stall with him and swept the heavy brush along his back. He seemed to enjoy it.

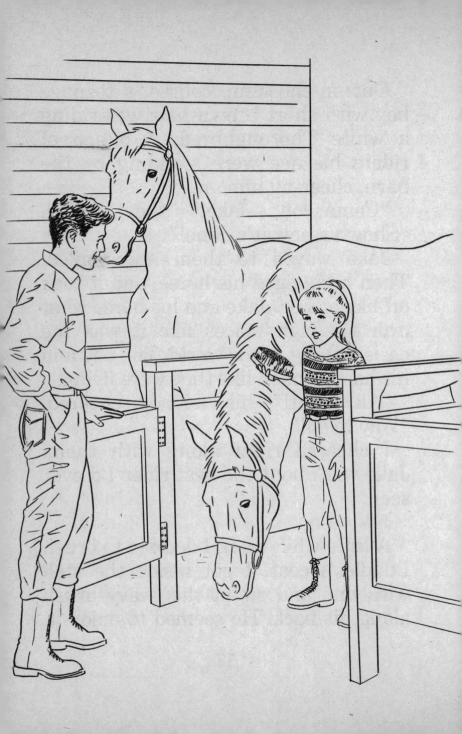

We were becoming friends again.

I heard a horse come inside the barn. When I looked up, I saw Jake leading his horse to a stall. "See you next time, Phantom," he said affectionately as he closed the latch.

As he was brushing the dust off his boots, he saw me looking at him. "Hi," he said. "I'm Jake." He had a nice smile.

"Hi. I'm Elizabeth," I said. "I saw you out there. You're really good."

"Thanks," he said. "Actually, Phantom does most of the work. You must ride, too, huh?"

I blushed. "Well, I used to," I said. "But I'm kind of afraid to now."

Jake frowned. "How come?"

"Well . . . I had a pretty bad fall."

Jake nodded. "That can be scary," he said.

"I bet you never fell off a horse," I said. "Since you're so good and everything."

He laughed. Then he took out a

sugar cube and gave it to Puddles.

"Why are you laughing?" I asked.

"I don't know," he said. "It's not even funny, really. Once, when I was about your age, I got thrown by a horse. It was bad. I broke my leg, my arm, a bunch of ribs . . ."

I stared. "You're kidding!" I said.

"I wouldn't kid about it, believe me," he said. "I was in the hospital for weeks. And when I got out, I had to have all kinds of physical therapy. It wasn't much fun. They said I'd never ride again."

I shivered. "If I got hurt that badly, I wouldn't *want* to," I said.

"I didn't either, at first," Jake said. "But after a while I just missed horses. So I kept doing my exercises, and eventually I was able to get back in the saddle."

"Weren't you scared?"

Jake shrugged. "At first," he said. "But I got over it."

Puddles finished the sugar cube and licked Jake's hand. "That's a beautiful horse you've got here," Jake said.

Puddles snorted thank you.

"I think he wants another sugar cube," I said with a laugh.

Jake ruffled Puddles's mane and gave him more sugar. "Now, you do what Elizabeth says, OK?" he told Puddles. "Good horse."

We heard a car horn. "That's my ride," Jake said. "Nice talking to you, Elizabeth."

"Nice talking to you, too," I said.

He started to leave. Just as he got to the door, he turned.

"Are you riding in the horse show this weekend?" he asked.

"I'm supposed to," I said.

Jake nodded. "Bet you win a ribbon," he said. Then he smiled and went out the door.

CHAPTER 10

Little Girl on a Big Horse

After Jake left, I started thinking. He really almost had been killed—but he was riding better than ever!

Jake must be really brave, I thought. *A lot braver than me.*

And yet Jake thought I could get back in the saddle, too. Even though he hardly knew me at all, he had more faith in me than I did.

Puddles fidgeted in the stall, shifting his weight from one leg to another. The poor horse had been cooped up for days, just because I was afraid to ride.

I thought about how happy and

graceful Jake had looked on his horse. You could tell he really loved to gallop and feel the wind in his face. Jake and Phantom had moved like they were one big graceful animal.

Suddenly I realized how much I missed riding. There was nothing like the feeling of flying across the field on the back of a horse. It was so much fun—what could have ever convinced me to stop?

I was lost in my daydream when I heard someone yell from the ring.

"Easy, horsey! No!"

It sounded like someone was in trouble. I went and looked out the back door of the barn.

There was the same little girl I'd seen before, on top of her huge black Thoroughbred. The horse kept kicking the ground and shaking his head. The girl didn't have control of him at all.

Just then, the girl's riding instructor

came around the corner of the barn. He ran toward the Thoroughbred.

"Jamie!" he yelled. "I told you not to take Ebony out of the stall until I came back!"

"It's OK," Jamie said, though she looked pretty scared. "I can handle him OK, really! Watch."

Jamie kicked the horse in the side with the heels of her boots. I guess it was the wrong thing to do, because Ebony took off like a shot.

"Help!" Jamie screamed. She held on for dear life as Ebony ran to the fence and jumped right over it. Chills crept up my spine. I knew how scared she must be.

"Hang on, Jamie!" the instructor shouted. He turned to me. "What am I going to do? Somebody else has my horse!" He ran off to get help.

"Wait!" I shouted. "My horse is right—"

But he couldn't hear me. I looked and saw the little girl bouncing on the Thoroughbred's back. By the time the instructor got another horse, they might both be across the field and into the woods. She could really get hurt!

I looked back inside the barn. Puddles had heard the commotion. He gave me a curious look and scraped the ground with his right front hoof.

"All right, Puddles," I said. I ran inside, put on my riding hat, unlatched his gate, and grabbed his reins. "It's time to ride!"

CHAPTER 11

To the Rescue!

When I led Puddles out of the barn, we saw the black Thoroughbred galloping across the field. Puddles snorted and clomped the ground. He was raring to go.

I took a deep breath, closed my eyes, and swung myself up into the saddle. There was no time to be scared.

"Come on, Puddles!" I shouted. "Go get 'em!"

Puddles broke right into a fast gallop, as if he'd been waiting for a chance to run free. We were flying. I kept my legs tight around Puddles and held on.

We were racing fast toward the fence. "We'll have to jump it, Puddles!" I cried. "Can you do it?"

Puddles snorted, put his head down, and galloped even faster. My horse had more nerve than I did. I just swallowed hard and tried not to think about what would happen to us if we didn't make it.

We were going so fast, my hair streamed behind me in the wind. The fence was twenty feet away—then fifteen—then *ten*—

"Now!" I shouted, and Puddles leaped. It seemed like we were in the air for a long time. The sun struck my eyes and for a second I was blinded.

Then I felt Puddles hit the ground with his front hooves. We had cleared the fence.

"All right, Puddles!" I yelled. I slapped him on the behind. "I knew you could do it!"

The black Thoroughbred was about two hundred yards ahead of us. He wasn't running in a straight line, but zigzagging across the field toward the woods. I saw the little girl on his back, hanging on to his mane as tight as she could. "Help me, somebody!" she screamed. She was starting to slide out of the saddle.

I rode Puddles on at top speed. He was running fast and steady. I realized I had never ridden so fast on a horse before. It was really exciting!

The Thoroughbred must have been slowing down, because we were gaining on it. "Hang on, Jamie!" I called to the little girl. "We're coming!"

"Hurry!" Jamie cried. She sounded terrified.

Before I knew it, we were right

behind the Thoroughbred. I steered Puddles so that he was running alongside the other horse. I could see that Jamie was losing her grip on the Thoroughbred's mane. I wasn't sure I could save her before she fell.

Jamie looked at me with fear in her eyes. "Stop him!"

"Just hold on tight!" I told her. "You'll be fine!"

I needed to get a hold of the Thoroughbred's reins. They were flapping loose from his neck. I kept my own reins in my left hand and reached over with my right. I missed.

I looked ahead. The trees were coming up fast!

Don't be afraid, I told myself. *You can do it.*

I kept my eyes on the loose reins. When they swung toward me, I reached my hand out for them. I caught them!

"Whoa!" I called. "Whoa, Puddles!" And I pulled on Puddles's and the Thoroughbred's reins at the same time. Puddles slowed to a stop. A second later, the Thoroughbred stopped, too. I felt like he'd stretched my right arm out a few inches, but we were all safe. Whew!

The little girl still held on to her horse's mane. She was shaking. "Th-thank you," she said. "Could you help me down?"

"Sure!" I said. I jumped down to the ground and gave Jamie a hand. "Are you all right?"

"Y-yeah," Jamie said. "I guess so. I was scared."

"I don't blame you," I said. "I would have been scared, too."

I knew how it felt to be scared.

We heard hoofbeats. Jamie's

instructor came galloping over on a brown horse. Amy and Becky were riding behind him.

Jamie's instructor dismounted and ran up to her. "Thank goodness you're all right!" he said. Then he turned to me. "We saw how you saved her. Nice going."

I blushed. "Anyone would have done it," I said.

"Jamie, next time, *please* don't get on the horse unless I'm there, OK?" her instructor said.

Jamie shivered and hugged herself. "There isn't going to *be* a next time," she said. "I'm never getting on a horse again."

Jamie and I looked at each other. I knew what I had to do.

"Don't give it up," I said. "Just because you had a little scare doesn't mean riding isn't fun, right?"

"That's easy for you to say," Jamie

answered. "You're a great rider. I can hardly ride at all."

"That's not true," I said. "A couple of weeks ago, I was thrown by a horse."

Jamie's mouth dropped open. "Really?"

"Really," I said. "And I said I'd never ride again. But I finally got over it."

"Wow," Jamie said. She didn't look quite so afraid anymore. "Maybe you're right." She went over and stood beside the Thoroughbred. I could see she was a little afraid of him, but she didn't let that stop her. She took hold of his reins. Then she looked over her shoulder and smiled at me. "What's your name?" she asked.

"Elizabeth," I told her.

"Nice to meet you, Elizabeth," Jamie said. "Thanks again."

"Don't mention it."

"Come on, Jamie," her instructor said. "Let's put Ebony back in the barn."

Jamie and her instructor walked off together. As I got back into the saddle, Becky gave me a serious look.

"You know you shouldn't have gone after Jamie by yourself, don't you, Elizabeth?" she asked. "You could have put yourself in real danger."

I looked at the ground and nodded.

But when I looked up, Becky's face had broken into a smile. "But I can't help feeling really proud of you, too. That was a very, very brave thing you did."

"We saw you from the barn," Amy said excitedly. "I can't believe you jumped that fence!"

"Puddles did most of the work," I said. I patted his neck. He whinnied happily. We were a team again.

"Do we still have time to practice for the show?" I asked Becky.

CHAPTER 12

Back in the Saddle

The day of the Happy Hoofs Horse Show, I sat on Puddles's back, wearing my riding pants, a pretty ruffled shirt, and my riding hat. Puddles was wearing a brand-new red bow in his mane. A big crowd of parents and friends sat on folding chairs at the edge of the field. I could see Mom, Dad, Jessica, Grandma, Grandpa, and Great-aunt Helen. They announced my name, and Puddles and I rode out to the center of the ring. When we came to a fence, Puddles jumped gracefully over it. I smiled and waved to the audience. I could hear the crowd applaud.

After two more riders performed, the time came for the man to announce the winners. Amy and the other kids in our category stood next to our horses.

"First place in this event goes to . . . Elizabeth Wakefield!" said a man wearing a big top hat.

I felt a flutter of excitement in my stomach as I led Puddles to the stage to collect my award. Everybody applauded and cheered. I could see my family. They were beaming. I was so happy, I forgot to be embarrassed.

"And in second place," the man went on, "Amy Sutton!"

Everyone clapped. I clapped, too. The man gave Amy her red ribbon.

"I'll get you in the next event," she whispered in my ear.

I grinned. "We'll see about that," I whispered back. We laughed. It felt good to be riding pals again.

Amy held her ribbon up to mine. "Wait'll Jerry gets a look at these!" she said.

I nodded. I was looking forward to that myself.

In between events, I went over to give Grandma, Grandpa, and Great-aunt Helen hugs. They had dressed up for the occasion, and Great-aunt Helen wore a flowery pink hat over her silver hair.

"There's my little champion!" Great-aunt Helen said, squeezing me tight.

"Puddles is the real champ," I said. "I just sat on him."

"Don't you give the horse *all* the credit!" Grandpa said. "Anyone can see that you're one of the best riders out there."

"No kidding!" Jessica said. "I bet after saving that girl's life, riding Puddles around some obstacle course was no sweat, huh?"

"We're all very proud of you, Elizabeth," Mom said.

"We certainly are!" Grandma said, hugging me again.

"Especially me!" Jessica said.

Right then, out of the corner of my eye, I saw Jake. He was standing by the fence. He winked at me.

"I'll be right back," I said to my family.

Jake was smiling as I came up to him. "Hi, Elizabeth," he said. "Great job. I knew you'd win a ribbon."

"Thanks," I said. "Actually, I have another thing to thank you for."

"What's that?" he asked. His eyebrows arched up.

"For helping me get my courage back," I said.

"You didn't need my help to be brave," he said. "You saved that girl all by yourself! Give yourself some credit, champ!"

"Elizabeth!" It was Becky calling to me. She waved me over to the barn. "Hurry up, or you'll miss the next event!"

"OK!" I shook Jake's hand. "Thanks again," I said.

"No problem," Jake said. "Just go win another ribbon, OK?"

"OK!"

I ran over to the door of the barn. "I've got a surprise for you." Becky smiled.

"What?" I said.

Becky stepped aside, and I saw Jamie, leading Puddles out of the barn.

"Jamie!" I said. "I didn't know you were going to be here!"

"I asked my mom to bring me, so

I could watch you compete," she said. "Besides, I want to win one of those someday." She pointed to my ribbon.

"I'm sure you will," I said.

Jamie handed Puddles's reins over to me. He looked more beautiful than ever. I'd brushed his coat until it shone. His mane was braided, just like my ponytail. When he saw me coming, Puddles threw back his head and made a horsey sound that reminded me of a laugh.

"I know just how you feel, boy," I said. I jumped into the saddle. And I knew I was right where I belonged.

That night Grandma, Grandpa, and Great-aunt Helen joined us for a big celebration dinner at Munchy's Restaurant. Jessica and I had our favorite ice-cream sundaes for dessert—strawberry and chocolate with lots of whipped cream and sprinkles.

"I can't get over what a great job you did in the horse show today," Great-aunt Helen said. "I would have been scared to ride such a big horse."

Jessica, Mom, and I winked at one another.

"It was a piece of cake," I said.

"Now since Elizabeth is a blue-ribbon rider, I'd like to announce that I've signed up Steven for some lessons of his own," said Mom.

"Really? What kind of lessons?" Steven asked. "Scuba diving? Baseball? Parasailing?"

"None of those," Mom said, smiling mysteriously.

"Then it's got to be hockey. I can see it now—I'm sliding across the ice with the puck about to hit a goal . . ."

"No, it's not hockey," Mom said. "I'll give you a hint. You'll have to wear a tie."

"A tie?" Steven said. "What kind of sport can that be?"

"It's not a sport," said Mom. "It's an activity."

"You're going to give me waiter lessons?" asked Steven. Everyone at our table started to laugh. But Steven didn't look too happy.

"Maybe Steven's going to learn how to be a teacher!" Jessica said, giggling.

"Be quiet, know-it-all," Steven said.

"That's all I'm going to tell you," Mom said. "But I think you'll enjoy it."

"If I'm going to have to wear a tie, I don't think I'm going to enjoy it," said Steven, slumping in his chair.

What kind of lessons has Mrs. Wakefield signed Steven up for? Find out in Sweet Valley Kids #65, **STEVEN'S BIG CRUSH.**

SIGN UP FOR THE SWEET VALLEY HIGH® FAN CLUB!

Hey, girls! Get all the gossip on Sweet Valley High's® most popular teenagers when you join our fantastic Fan Club! As a member, you'll get all of this really cool stuff:

- Membership Card with your own personal Fan Club ID number
- A Sweet Valley High® Secret Treasure Box
- Sweet Valley High® Stationery
- Official Fan Club Pencil (for secret note writing!)
- Three Bookmarks
- A "Members Only" Door Hanger
- Two Skeins of J. & P. Coats® Embroidery Floss with flower barrette instruction leaflet
- Two editions of *The Oracle* newsletter
- Plus exclusive Sweet Valley High® product offers, special savings, contests, and much more!

Be the first to find out what Jessica & Elizabeth Wakefield are up to by joining the Sweet Valley High® Fan Club for the one-year membership fee of only $6.25 each for U.S. residents, $8.25 for Canadian residents (U.S. currency). Includes shipping & handling.

Send a check or money order (do not send cash) made payable to "Sweet Valley High® Fan Club" along with this form to:

SWEET VALLEY HIGH® FAN CLUB, BOX 3919-B, SCHAUMBURG, IL 60168-3919

NAME _____
(Please print clearly)

ADDRESS _____

CITY_____ STATE _____ ZIP_____
(Required)

AGE _____ BIRTHDAY_____ /_____ /_____

Offer good while supplies last. Allow 6-8 weeks after check clearance for delivery. Addresses without ZIP codes cannot be honored. Offer good in USA & Canada only. Void where prohibited by law.
©1993 by Francine Pascal   LCI-1383-123

SWEET VALLEY KIDS

Jessica and Elizabeth have had lots of adventures in *Sweet Valley High* and *Sweet Valley Twins*...now read about the twins at age seven! You'll love all the fun that comes with being seven—birthday parties, playing dress-up, class projects, putting on puppet shows and plays, losing a tooth, setting up lemonade stands, caring for animals and much more! It's all part of SWEET VALLEY KIDS. Read them all!

☐	JESSICA AND THE SPELLING-BEE SURPRISE #21	15917-8	$2.99
☐	SWEET VALLEY SLUMBER PARTY #22	15934-8	$2.99
☐	LILA'S HAUNTED HOUSE PARTY # 23	15919-4	$2.99
☐	COUSIN KELLY'S FAMILY SECRET # 24	15920-8	$2.99
☐	LEFT-OUT ELIZABETH # 25	15921-6	$2.99
☐	JESSICA'S SNOBBY CLUB # 26	15922-4	$2.99
☐	THE SWEET VALLEY CLEANUP TEAM # 27	15923-2	$2.99
☐	ELIZABETH MEETS HER HERO #28	15924-0	$2.99
☐	ANDY AND THE ALIEN # 29	15925-9	$2.99
☐	JESSICA'S UNBURIED TREASURE # 30	15926-7	$2.99
☐	ELIZABETH AND JESSICA RUN AWAY # 31	48004-9	$2.99
☐	LEFT BACK! #32	48005-7	$2.99
☐	CAROLINE'S HALLOWEEN SPELL # 33	48006-5	$2.99
☐	THE BEST THANKSGIVING EVER # 34	48007-3	$2.99
☐	ELIZABETH'S BROKEN ARM # 35	48009-X	$2.99
☐	ELIZABETH'S VIDEO FEVER # 36	48010-3	$2.99
☐	THE BIG RACE # 37	48011-1	$2.99
☐	GOODBYE, EVA? # 38	48012-X	$2.99
☐	ELLEN IS HOME ALONE # 39	48013-8	$2.99
☐	ROBIN IN THE MIDDLE #40	48014-6	$2.99
☐	THE MISSING TEA SET # 41	48015-4	$2.99
☐	JESSICA'S MONSTER NIGHTMARE # 42	48008-1	$2.99
☐	JESSICA GETS SPOOKED # 43	48094-4	$2.99
☐	THE TWINS BIG POW-WOW # 44	48098-7	$2.99
☐	ELIZABETH'S PIANO LESSONS # 45	48102-9	$2.99

A BANTAM SKYLARK BOOK

FRANCINE PASCAL'S

SWEET VALLEY Twins AND FRIENDS.®